THE FAMOUS FIVE

ANNUAL 2016

BOOKS IN THE FAMOUS FIVE SERIES

All available from Hodder Children's books

THE
FAMOUS
FIVE

ANNUAL 2016

*Hodder
Children's
Books*

A division of Hachette Children's Group

With special thanks – for the third year running – to Tony Summerfield of the Enid Blyton Society for advice and contributions to this book. For more information about the Famous Five and the world of Enid Blyton, visit www.enidblytonsociety.co.uk

First published in Great Britain in 2015 by Hodder Children's Books

A Catalogue record for this book is available from the British Library

ISBN 978 1 444 92713 9

Book design by Janette Revill
Printed and bound in China

The paper and board used in this hardback by Hodder Children's Books are natural recyclable products made from wood grown in sustainable forests. The manufacturing processes conform to the environmental regulations of the country of origin.

Hodder Children's Books
a division of Hachette Children's Group
Part of Hodder & Stoughton
Carmelite House, 50 Victoria Embankment,
London, EC4Y 0DZ
An Hachette UK company

www.hachette.co.uk

ACKNOWLEDGEMENTS

'The Famous Five Play', 'Finniston Farm Revisited!', 'The Famous Five Musical', 'What's Wrong?' and 'The Famous Five in America' are all written by Tony Summerfield, who also supplied the photographs to illustrate the play.

'Caves, Secret Passages and Tunnels', 'Two Famous Pastimes', 'A Tour Round Kirrin Island', 'Castles and Other Buildings' and the 'Fiendish Famous Five Quiz' are all written by Norman Wright, and were first published in *The Famous Five: Everything You Ever Wanted to Know*.

'Which Famous Five Book Should I Read Next?', 'Which Character Are You?' and 'Ladder to a Baddie' are all by Anita Bensoussane.

The illustrations from *Well Done, Famous Five* are by Jamie Littler, from the Famous Five Colour Short Stories edition of the same title.

The image on p 40 was created as marketing material for the Film Centre International Ltd.

'Up On the Moors' is an extract from *Five Go Off to Camp*, a *Famous Five Annual*, published by Purnell in 1984, which also includes the artwork for 'Mr Luffy's Fruitcake'.

'Happy Christmas, Five' first appeared in *The Famous Five Annual*, published by Grandreams Ltd.

The map of Kirrin Island on p. 35 is by Gillian Clements and was first published in *The Famous Five: Everything You Ever Wanted to Know*, by Hodder Children's Books, in 2000.

The photograph which accompanies the 'Hidden Messages' puzzle on p. 35 is courtesy of Coolabi.

The cover from *Enid Blyton's Adventure Magazine No 3* was published by Guttenburghus under licence from Darrel Waters Ltd in 1986. 'Island of Danger' is from issue 1 (1985), as is the extract from *Five On Kirrin Island Again*. The extract from *Five Go Adventuring Again* is from issue 15.

CONTENTS

THE FAMOUS FIVE AND ME:

Hilary McKay, a fan and author, writes . . .

Oh yes. Those twenty-one sunlit epics. Julian, Dick, George and Anne and Timmy the dog.

How I loved them.

Loved? What am I concealing here?

Love! I love them yet.

But first things first, we must get this out of the way, so that our relationship can be complete, no niggling grudges to cloud the bright Enid skies:

IT ISN'T FAIR.

ISN'T AND WASN'T AND NEVER WILL BE FAIR.

I don't know about other readers than me (I believe there were others) but I, as the D'Artagnan in this long love affair, was handicapped from the start.

Not only did I not possess an island of my own, a castle on that island, dungeons belonging to that castle, gold ingots (I beg your pardon? Ingots? Oh, ingots. Those things. Of course I knew. Just took me by surprise. Ingots, ingots, ingots, got it now) piled in heaps in my castle dungeons, a rowing boat with which to reach the castle, a perfect dog (Timmy), a loyal fisher boy (what's one of them?) with whom to lodge my perfect dog, a spectacular

scientist father from whom to hide the perfect dog, a downtrodden yet adorable mother (Why did she marry the scientist father? Why was she never allowed to meet his relations until they dumped all three children on her to stay for the summer? Was she a secret feminist? I think she was: she insisted that her husband take her name upon marriage [don't believe me? Check it out! Kirrin Cottage? Kirrin Island? Which she gave to her primary school aged daughter before our story commences.] [Why, Aunt Fanny, would you do that, anyway? If I had an island I would KEEP it for myself.])

Five On Finniston Farm

But I digress (waist deep in brackets) so back to the ISN'T AND WASN'T AND NEVER WILL BE FAIR.

My parents never ever let me go off in a horse drawn caravan with my friends.

Not once.

Not for one night.

Ever.

NOT because they couldn't afford a horse or a caravan (they couldn't, but even if they could, they wouldn't).

NOT because the idea never occurred to them. (It did. I caused it to occur very often.)

Because (and I quote) they thought it *a silly idea.*

That's what they said.

AND ...

When I was very ill and pale and weak from influenza, what happened? A Welsh Cottage in the snowy Alps? Driven there by private chauffeur? School told not to expect me for ages and ages?

Alas.

I think not.

Nothing like.

Multivits, a smearing of Vick and a toilet roll for my nose.

AND that's not all.

Why wasn't I ever let out to hobnob with circus boys?

Where was my wicked tutor when I failed my exams?

What happened to my due ration of kindly farmers' wives, eager to stuff me with raspberries and cream and hard boiled eggs and enormous hams and ginger cake and whacking great salads? I never, in my whole hungry childhood, met one.

Also, my lighthouse? My castle walls? My cave with my heather bed? My bicycle with the magic panniers stuffed full of frying pans, sketch books, warm blankets, tents and swimming kit? I'd like them now, please, I've waited long enough.

And, let us not underestimate the homesickness.

I was born in a red brick end of terrace, very close to the gas works. I played in a street of black tar and knife-sharp gravel. There was a severe shortage of grass in every direction.

I ached for my landscape. Oh, the purple heather moors, bright seas, silvery coves and golden gorse of my story book youth!

Was it fair?
No.
AND FINALLY …
My baddies!
Those charismatic folk with the strange accents, misfiring revolvers, secret night time light spectaculars, lank hair, short tempers, inability to differentiate between the male and female youthful form, EVEN WORSE ability to differentiate between the male and female youthful form thus sealing their fate with my good friend George/ina) AND BEST OF ALL(drumroll, because it saved the day so often)

… abject fear of brown mongrel dogs (TIMMY!).

I LIKED those baddies. I could (with my twenty-one instruction books) have coped with those baddies. They were nothing like the rotten pencil-case stealing, table tennis bat whacking (Hello, Miss Read!), school report writing baddies of my own hard life.

And yet, back to the beginning, to the Famous Five and Me.

Those books were lights. They were beacons. They were sign posts. They were an alternative world to which I could escape. They were friends and hope and comfort and the promise of all brightness on the horizon.

No wonder I loved them.

I love them yet.

Hilary McKay is the Whitbread Award-winning author of *Saffy's Angel* and other books about the Casson Family. Her new novel, *Binny in Secret*, is out now and is perfect for fans of Enid Blyton's family stories.

THE FAMOUS FIVE PLAY

Enid Blyton used her two-page fortnightly letter in *Enid Blyton's Magazine* to both thank children for things that they had done and things that they had sent her and also as a place to talk about new books and serials that were about to get published. It was also a place for any news on forthcoming events. On 11 May 1955 she had an exciting announcement for her many Famous Five readers ...

'Now I have a piece of news for you again – I have written a Famous Five play at last! The lovers of Noddy had their wish, for I wrote the play *Noddy in Toyland* for them, which thousands of you saw last Christmas – and you will be able to see again next Christmas too. Now it is the turn of the older children who begged me for a Famous Five play so that they too could have one of their own to see, not only in London, but in all the big towns of the kingdom. So I have written it for you. It is called *Famous Five Adventure*, and it has Kirrin Cottage in it, and a Fair, and Kirrin Island too – *and* the Castle with its dungeons! It is what you asked me to make it – funny – exciting – and real! And Timmy the dog is in it – imagine that! But he is my main difficulty. You see, we cannot have the real Timmy of course – so I have to look about for one as like him as possible – and he must be a clever dog too, because he has a certain amount of

acting to do. I shall see plenty of dogs, I expect, before I choose a Timmy. But won't it be exciting, children, to see the Famous Five on the stage, all alive and merry and bright! I shall be as excited as you when I first see *Famous Five Adventure*.'

Over the next few months the play got several more mentions with auditions starting in June ('dozens and dozens of children') in which Enid herself took an active part and later the anticipated difficulties of trying to find a suitable Timmy, with all creatures great and small arriving for Enid to inspect. On 7 December, Enid wrote that 'We have a tall and determined Julian, you'll like him (Gordon Gardner). Dick is shorter and a real joker (Michael Maguire), Anne is her usual gentle friendly self (Janice Edgard) – and George is what she is in the books – quick-tempered, impatient, loyal and brave (Pat Garwood). As for Timmy – well, you must wait till you see *him*!'

Gordon Gardner, Michael Maguire, Grazyna Frame and Pat Garwood in "The Famous Five" at the London Hippodrome.

Enid had said that the play was 'a new adventure – but just a little bit like one or two of the books.' This was possibly an understatement as the plot was very similar to her latest book, *Five Have Plenty of Fun*, which had been published in July. In both cases the family is asked to look after a child of an American colleague of Uncle Quentin's called Elbur who is afraid that his child is about to be kidnapped. In the book this is a daughter called Berta and in the play a son called Junior. In both versions George ends up being kidnapped by mistake.

Enid told her readers exactly which box she would be sitting in at the theatre so that children could wave at her and she would wave back, although she might not be present at all

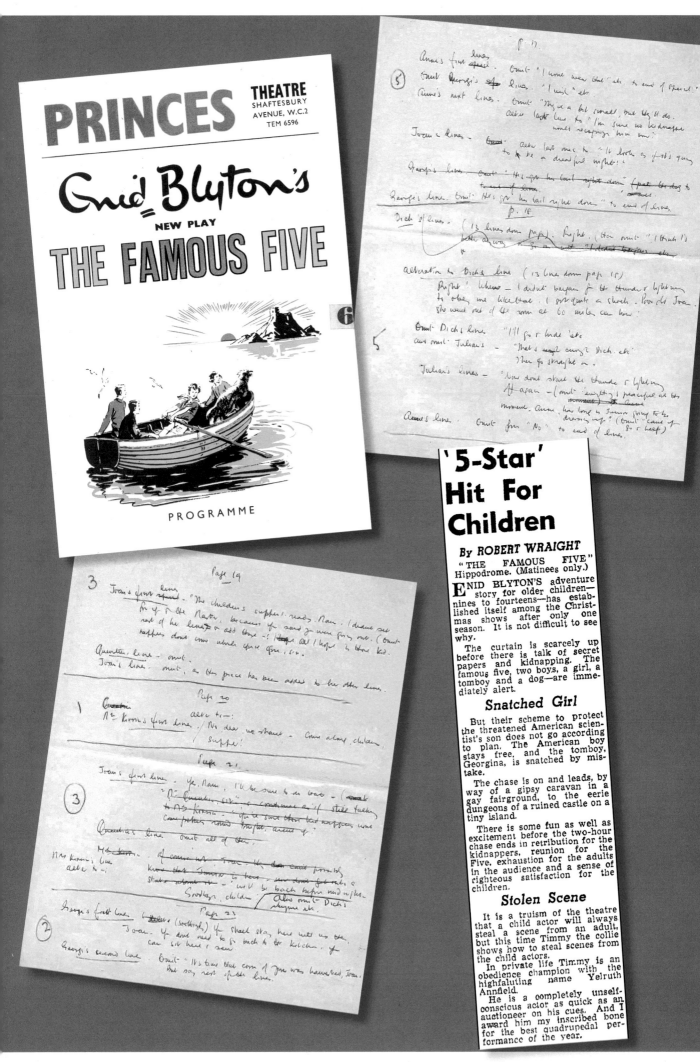

Enid Blyton,
Green Hedges,
Penn Road,
Beaconsfield,
Telephone : Beaconsfield 1091. Bucks.

Famous Five Adventure.

A Play for Older Children.

In Three Acts.

By Only Carbon of Working Script with all additions & alterations. also Andre suggestions Nov 14

Characters.

The "Famous Five"
(Julian)
(Dick) brothers and sister.
(Anne)
Georgina, who is always called George. Cousin to above three)
Timmy, George's dog.
Mr. Quentin Kirrin (George's father, and uncle to the others)
Mrs. Kirrin ...... (George's mother, and Aunt Fanny to the others).
Joan .... (the cook and general friend of the family).
Mr. Elbur .... (An American scientist, friend of Mr. Kirrin.)
Junior .... (his son)
Polly Boswell .... (a gypsy girl from the Fair)
Mr. Strong-Man Jake (strong man at Fair)
Mrs. Jake .... (his wife)
Bob .... (hoopla boy) (coconut-shy boy)
George Boswell ... (Polly's uncle)
Max ....) kidnappers
Ike ....)
The boss .... (master of above two)
Dan .....) sailors on Boss's motor-launch.
Bill .....)
Rod ......
Inspector of Police.
Police Sergeant.
One (or two) Constables.
Two or three odd people at Fair.
(Note: A good deal of doubling can be carried out)

performances! She also said that both she and the cast would like it if they all wore their Famous Five Club badges.

Famous Five Adventure opened at Princes Theatre in Shaftesbury Avenue on 23 December 1955. It shared the theatre with *Noddy in Toyland* which was performed as a matinee at 2.30, with the Famous Five on stage at 7.15 each evening ('how grown-up!' said Enid in her letter on 21 December 21). As both plays involved a number of scene changes this must have proved an absolute nightmare for the poor stage hands. Some of the adult actors appeared in both plays and Ronnie Corbett remarked in his autobiography that he was in Noddy in the afternoon and the Famous Five in the evening. Andre van Gyseghem was the director of both plays.

On 1 February 1956 Enid said in her *Magazine* letter that, 'The play was such a tremendous success that it will certainly be on again, so if you didn't see it you will be able to do so another

time.' Her initial announcement of the play, when she said that children could see it 'not only in London, but in all the big towns of the kingdom', never came to fruition as it didn't go on tour, but she was right in saying that it would be on again as it came back to London in the following year.

This time it did not share a theatre with Noddy, who went back to the Stoll Theatre in Kingsway, which was the original theatre that he had been in back in 1954. The Famous Five opened at the London Hippodrome in Leicester Square on 20 December 1956. It was not quite so 'grown-up' this time as it was just for a 2.30 matinee each day. Three of the children, Julian, Dick and George, were played by the same actors, but the role of Anne was played by Grazyna Frame. It had some good reviews, but once again did not go on tour and this time when it closed, it closed for good as it was never performed again and there was a forty year gap until the Famous Five took to the stage once more, but that is another story!

ACT 1
Scene 1

(Kirrin Cottage. An ordinary and pleasant living-room, with comfortable chairs about and a couch. Also a table big enough for meals. The room looks as if it is lived in, for there are papers here and there, some on the floor, and half-open books on the couch. A jigsaw puzzle, half-finished, is on the table. Vases of flowers are here and there. A jersey is flung over a chair-back, and a hat or cap is on the floor.

At the back is a very big, wide window, opening on to a view of the sea, for the house faces Kirrin Bay. The room is full of sunlight, very bright and pleasant. In the distance (on the back-cloth) is Kirrin Island, which lies at the entrance to Kirrin Bay. This is a small island, rather bare and sandy, but with a most romantic -looking, ruined stone castle in the middle.

There are three doors – one left, one right, and a third, back stage left, which is a glass French window, flush with the wide windows. This glass door opens on a small garden whose gate leads almost directly on the beach. A small lane is supposed to divide garden from beach.

As the cottage is so near the beach, the sound of waves and cries of gulls can be heard at times, but not in such a way as to interfere with the speaking.

The stage is empty when the curtain goes up. The sound of the sea can be heard, and two or three gulls calling. Almost immediately JOAN, the cook, enters, tray in hand. She is a buxom, bustling, cheerful woman, good-humoured but sharp-tongued.

It is a summer evening.

(JOAN Hums loudly as she proceeds to set the table for a light supper. She bangs about a bit with plates etc. Then she begins to sing loudly but not tunefully, and finally proceeds to drop the big tin tray with a clatter on to her foot. She sinks down into a chair and groans.)

JOAN: Ooooh! My corn! Dropped the tray right on it. Ooooooh!

(Door in left opens suddenly and QUENTIN KIRRIN *George's Father and uncle to the other three children comes half in, looking furious.*)

QUENTIN: (*angry*) What's this awful row going on? How many times have I said that I MUST HAVE QUIET when I work?

JOAN: Sorry, Sir. It was only me singing - and then I dropped the tray on my corn. Ooooh! (*bends down to foot, twists it about etc.*)

QUENTIN: Singing! Do you call that singing, Joan? It nearly deafened <u>me</u> (*retires, banging study door loudly*)

JOAN: (*hands to ears*) OOOOOH - that door! It nearly deafened <u>me</u>!

(Enter MRS.KIRRIN, dishes in hand)

MRS. KIRRIN: What's all the noise about, Joan?

JOAN: Just the master banging the study door as usual, Mam. Oooh, my corn! I dropped the tray on it. (*stands up and begins to limp to table again.*) Oooooh!

MRS. KIRRIN:You and your corn, Joan! (*helps JOAN lay table*) I suppose the noise of the tray brought the Master out of the study as usual. He's been working very hard, you know.

JOAN: Yes, Mam, I know. I can't even sing without him coming out and shouting at me (*drops two or three knives and forks*puts hand to mouth and looks fearfully at study door.*)

MRS. KIRRIN:(*laughing*) Pick them up, Joan. He didn't hear. I'm thankful that his last big scientific job is over, and all the figures are finished and checked.

JOAN: He's been working with that famous American scientist, hasn't he, Mam - what's his name now?

MRS. KIRRIN:Elbur - Mr. Elbur. Yes, they've done a wonderful piece of work together - and now it's finished perhaps the Master will take things a bit easy.

JOAN: I'm sure I hope so - popping in and out of that study like a jack-in-the-box every time anyone—

(As JOAN speaks someone comes up to French window (the glass garden door) at back stage and rings the door-bell loud and long. It shrills out so suddenly that it makes JOAN and Mrs. KIRRIN jump. It rings again and again as if the visitor is extremely impatient)

JOAN: (*cross*) Now then, now then – who's in such a hurry!

(Once more the study door flies open, and QUENTIN stands there, hair on end)

QUENTIN: (*almost bellowing*) For pity's sake, ANSWER THAT BELL! How am I to work if …

MRS. KIRRIN:Now, now, Quentin, don't get so upset <u>please.</u>

(JOAN has gone to door as the bell rings again and the visitor also knocks on glass door with his knuckles. She opens it and MR. ELBUR strides in at once. He flings hat down, not seeing QUENTIN or his wife at first, only JOAN and appears to be very distraught)

ELBUR: Where's your master? Tell him I want to speak to him – urgently! Hurry, woman, hurry!

CAVES, SECRET PASSAGES AND TUNNELS

Where better to have an exciting adventure than deep beneath the ground, out of sight of interfering adults? Here are some of the locations which have led the Five into exciting endeavours …

Until *Five Run Away Together*, George believed that no caves existed on Kirrin Island. It was Dick who first spotted the cave as the Five were returning to the Island after exploring the old wreck. The cave entrance was almost completely hidden by rocks and only visible from one point on the shore. It has a floor of fine white sand and is perfectly dry. Round one side runs a rocky ledge on which the Five can store tins of food and spare torch batteries. A really useful feature of the cave is that it has a rooftop entrance leading up onto the cliff. This is partly hidden from above by bramble bushes. Julian tied a knotted rope round the roots of a large bush growing close by and the children used this to climb in and out of the cave.

On **Mystery Moor**, close to the deserted sand quarry, is a strange shaped hill honeycombed with passages and with a cave at the centre. Here Sniffer's father holds George and Anne captive in an attempt to find out what the two boys have done with packets of forged hundred-dollar bills that were dropped onto the moor by a low flying aircraft.

A network of caves close to **Billycock Hill** is open to the public. The entrance is properly paved and there is a large white noticeboard instructing visitors to keep to the rope-marked ways. Once through the two metre high entrance you are into the first of a series of small caves that lead to a large, magnificent cave full of what look like gleaming icicles. These are, in reality, stalagmites growing up from the cave floor and stalactites hanging down from the roof of the cave. The splendour of the place reminds Julian of being inside a cathedral. In places the stalagmites shine with all the colours of the rainbow and elsewhere they have formed so close together that they form 'a snow white screen'.

There are many forks and unmarked passages in the cave system and it is very easy for visitors who do not follow the marked routes to become lost. Jeff Thomas and Ray Wells are kept prisoner in one of the unexplored caves by foreign agents intent on stealing fighter aircraft from the air base close to **Billycock Hill.**

The entrance to the **Wreckers' Cave** at **Demon's Rocks** is through a large hole at the base of some very high cliffs. Lighted lanterns, set up by Jacob and Ebenezer Loomer, who guide visitors round the caves, shed a little light but inside the cave it is damp and cold with many large puddles in the floor that need to be avoided. Once inside, the tunnel twists round and leads downwards until you are walking under the sea itself and the noise of the ocean booming can be heard above your head. The tunnel eventually opens out into an extraordinary cave with a very high roof and irregular ridges running round the walls where the Wreckers once stored crates and boxes they stole from wrecked ships. From here there is a maze of tunnels that are flooded at high tide making them dangerous to explore.

Smuggler's Top, the old house built on the top of **Castaway Hill** in the middle of the marshes, has a number of secret passages which were originally used by smugglers. The entrance to the first one is close to the front door of the house and is useful for hiding Timmy from Mr Lenoir. Sooty Lenoir takes the children into an oak panelled room and presses the corner of one of the panels. A small part of the panel slides open. Inside is a lever which when pulled causes a large panel to open. The children and Timmy squeeze through into a narrow passage which eventually leads them to a cupboard in Sooty's bedroom. When he is not out walking with the children or being smuggled into one of their rooms Timmy has to live in this secret passage where he spends his time chasing rats! A second passage at Smuggler's Top begins in Marybelle's room. A trapdoor under the carpet leads down into a deep pit with passages leading off from it. The children use a rope ladder to descend into the pit but poor old Timmy has to be lowered down in a laundry basket. The third secret passage in the old house has its entrance in a window seat. This, like the passage in Marybelle's room, leads to the network of passages known as the Catacombs.

One of the most amazing secret passages used by the Five is that which runs under the bed of the ocean from Kirrin to Kirrin Island. One entrance can be found in the only near complete room left in Kirrin Castle. A stone in the fireplace recess can be swung open to reveal steps leading downwards through the thickness of the castle wall. The passage is very narrow at first but soon broadens out into a proper passage. This leads first to an enormous cave and then on to a

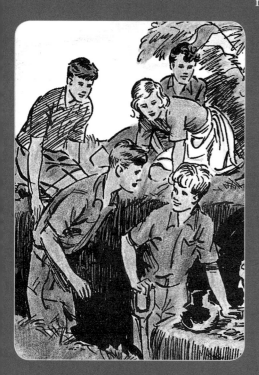

number of smaller caves. (Timmy was shut up in one of these by the villains in *Five on Kirrin Island Again*.) The passage then splits into three, and the left hand tunnel in turn again splits into three. Anyone not knowing their way could easily become lost in this maze of passages. If you do know the route and can negotiate the rock falls that have partly blocked the passage in places, the passage eventually leads to an entrance in the quarry on the moor behind Kirrin Cottage. Timmy successfully finds the route from the Island to the quarry and then takes Julian, Dick and Martin Curton back along it to Kirrin Island. Peters and Johnson, two villains trying to steal one of Quentin Kirrin's discoveries, get lost in the passages and Timmy has to be sent in to guide them out!

When Timmy gets tired of waiting outside **Faynights Castle** for the children to return from their visit he sniffs around looking for another way in and discovers the entrance to a secret passage that runs through the hollow wall of the castle. Part of the wall has crumbled leaving a small gap partway up the outer castle wall. The children follow Timmy's route and then squeeze through and find themselves in a low, narrow passage. They follow the passage and arrive at steps leading downwards. These lead to a wider, higher passage that turns off at right angles and leads them under the castle courtyard. A further flight of steps takes them to a small room, and a passage from this leads to spiral stairs going up into the remaining tower of the castle.

Have we missed any other secret caves, passages and tunnels? There are dozens in the Famous Five. Perhaps you could create your own mini-guide.

TWO FAMOUS PASTIMES

Camping

The very first cycling tour that the Five go on takes place during the Easter holidays in *Five Get Into Trouble*. They had been given two small tents for Christmas and, since the weather was so fine and their bikes were in tip top order, Aunt Fanny and Uncle Quentin give them permission to go for a cycling holiday. They fill their kit-bags with everything they will need: compass, map, sleeping bags, food, etc. and set off. They plan to cycle forty or fifty miles on their first day. They spend the first night camping close to the Green Pool and plan to spend the second in a flower-lined dell in Middlecombe Woods. But the adventure begins and they are soon off in search of **Owl's Dene**.

After getting annoyed at people laughing at Timmy when he has to wear a cardboard collar to stop him scratching the stitches in his ear, George goes off camping on Kirrin Common with him. She is later joined by Anne and finally the two boys join the group. They camp close to a ruined cottage and use a spring for water. Close by is a pool for bathing. Needless to say, the old cottage becomes the centre of a new adventure. You can read about this in *Five On a Secret Trail*.

The Five go camping on **Billycock Hill**, close to the farm where Toby Thomas lives. For their camping site they choose a spot halfway up the hill close to a spring and next to a giant gorse bush that will give them shelter and also a fine view.

George reckons that it is 'the best camp we've ever had.'

In their final adventure, the Five go to stay with Tinker Hayling and decide to camp in the field at the end of the garden where Tapper's Circus has set up camp. This is the easiest camping the Five have done as **Jenny,** the maid at **Big Hollow House,** prepares most of their food for them.

Caravanning

After watching a circus parade the children decide to go caravanning in *Five Go Off in a Caravan*. They borrow two modern, streamlined caravans and use Dobby, their own pony, to pull one

caravan and borrow the milkman's pony, Trotter, to pull the other. They set off for the Merran Hills where they have an exciting adventure with Nobby, the circus boy.

On their second caravan holiday (in *Five Have a Wonderful Time*) the Five borrow old-fashioned gypsy-style caravans that are parked in a field close to **Faynights Castle**. The boys' caravan is painted red with decorations in black and yellow, while the girls have a blue caravan with a design picked out in blue and yellow. The caravans have high wheels, a door at the front with steps up to it and a jutting roof with carving around the edge. The caravans have been modernised inside with folding-down bunk-beds, a little sink,

a small larder and shelves. A cork carpet helps to keep out the draughts.

The Five go caravanning and camp in a hollow in the Merran Hills sheltered from the wind. It is a peaceful place with birch trees close by, heather in abundance and hairbells growing in rock crevices. There is a rocky ledge where they can sit and eat their picnics overlooking Lake Merran. Anne calls the place Lake View. The lake is a splendid place for swimming with its sandy bottom and crystal clear water. They drink water from one of the many springs that gurgle from the hillside. A fast flowing stream that gushes out of the hillside is close by. The Five buy all the food they need from Farmer Mackie's wife.

WELL DONE, FAMOUS FIVE

Can you believe that sometimes the Five don't want to have an adventure? It's true – as you'll find out in this extract from one of the Famous Five short stories …

'Oh, for goodness' sake, don't wish for an adventure today!' said Anne. 'I like a bit of peace. I don't want to choke with excitement when I'm eating these delicious sandwiches! What *has* Aunt Fan put into them?'

'A bit of everything in the larder, I should think,' said George. 'Get away, Tim – don't breathe all over me like that!'

'What's that moving right away over there – along the side of that hill?' asked Dick, suddenly. 'Is it cows?'

Everyone looked. 'Too far away to see,' said George. 'Can't be cows, though – they don't move like cows – cows walk so slowly.'

'Well, they must be horses then,' said Julian.

'But who'd have so many horses out for exercise round here?' said George. 'All the horses are farm horses – they'd be working in the fields, not trotting in a row across a hillside.'

'It must be a riding school, idiot,' said Dick. 'If we had our binoculars, we'd see a lot of nicely behaved little girls from some nearby school cantering along on their nicely behaved horses!'

'I *did* bring my binoculars – didn't you notice?' said George, rummaging about behind her. 'I put them down here somewhere – ah, here they are. Want them, Dick?'

Dick took them and put them to his eyes. 'Yes – it's a line of horses – about six – wonderful ones too. But it's not girls who are riding them – it's boys – stable boys, I think.'

'Oh, of course – I forgot,' said George. 'They're wonderful racing horses from Lord Daniron's stable – they have to be exercised each day. Can you see a very big horse in the line, Dick? A magnificent creature – he's called Thunder-Along, and he's the most valuable horse in the country – so they say!'

Dick was now examining the horses with much interest, holding the binoculars to his eyes. 'They're *lovely* horses – and yes, I think I can see the one you mean, George. A great horse with a wonderful head – he's the first one of all.'

'Let me see,' said George, but Dick held on to the binoculars.

'No. Half a mo. Hey – something's happening! What is it? Something seemed to rush straight across in front of Thunder-Along – was it a fox or a dog? Oh, he's rearing up in fright, he's in quite a panic. He . . . He's off!' suddenly shouted Dick. 'He's thrown his groom – yes, he's on the ground, hurt, I think – and he's bolting! Oh no – he'll kill himself.'

A silence fell on the Five. Even Timmy was quiet, staring in the same direction as the others. George made as if to snatch her binoculars away from Dick, but he dodged, gluing them to his eyes.

'Don't lose sight of the horse, Dick, keep the binoculars on him,' said Julian, urgently. 'He's the finest horse this country has. Watch him – watch where he goes! We may be the only people who can see the way he takes.'

'All right, all right,' said Dick, impatiently. 'Don't jog my arm, Anne. Yes – there he goes – he's scared! He's still bolting at top speed – I hope he doesn't run into a tree – no, he just missed that one. Oh, now he's come to a gate – a high gate . . .'

Where will the horse end up? And will the Five – with their twelve legs! – be able to catch him up?

WHICH FAMOUS FIVE BOOK SHOULD I READ NEXT?

Try our quiz to see which Famous Five book might suit your current mood!

1 What kind of story do you like best?

A A story set in the countryside
B A story which takes place by the sea
C A tale full of atmosphere
D A creepy tale
E A story about a family

2 What would you want to see in a book?

A Animals
B Old legends
C Secret passages
D Happenings which seem impossible
E Long-lost treasure

3 Choose a descriptive word that appeals to you:

A Dreamy
B Old-fashioned
C Menacing
D Startling
E Wistful

4 Which activity would you prefer to do?

A Swim in a lake, pool or river
B Admire a wonderful view
C Explore an old town
D Go on a moorland hike
E Help to look after animals

5 Pick a weather condition that appeals to you:

A Warm and sunny
B Stormy
C Misty
D Breezy
E Hot and hazy

6 Which of these characters would you like to read about?

A People from a circus or fair
B Sea-faring folk
C A teacher or tutor
D People who live and work in the countryside
E Scientists or inventors

7 Which of these appeals to you most?

A Relaxation
B Tradition
C Progress
D Discovery
E Justice

8 Where would you prefer to stay if you went on holiday?

A In a caravan
B In a lighthouse
C In an old house
D In a tent
E On a farm

The answers are on page 64

FINNISTON FARM REVISITED!

In her biography of Enid Blyton, Barbara Stoney mentions a letter that Enid wrote to Noel Evans at Evans Brothers in 1949, and she quotes an extract of the letter that refers to Eileen Soper – whom we met in last year's *Annual* – as one of her main illustrators: 'I don't need to see roughs of any of her sketches. She and I have worked together for so long now and I have always found her accurate and most dependable – in fact excellent in every way . . .'

It would seem, however, that Enid was still keeping an eye on the Famous Five illustrations, as ten years after that letter she rejected at least two of the illustrations for *Five on Finniston Farm* and Eileen Soper was asked to redo them.

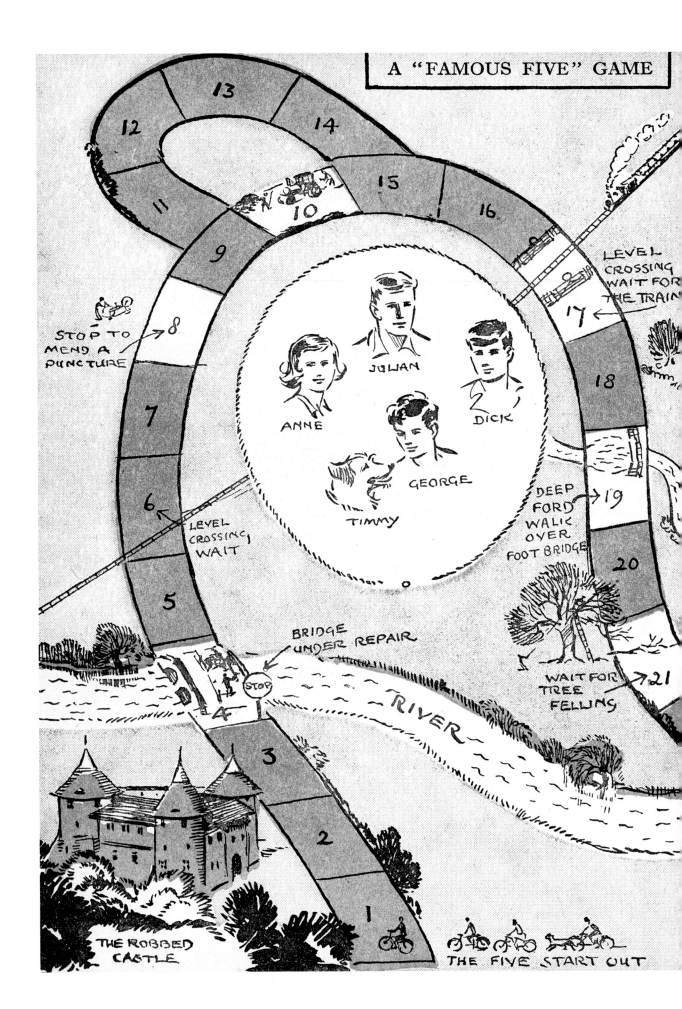

A "FAMOUS FIVE" GAME

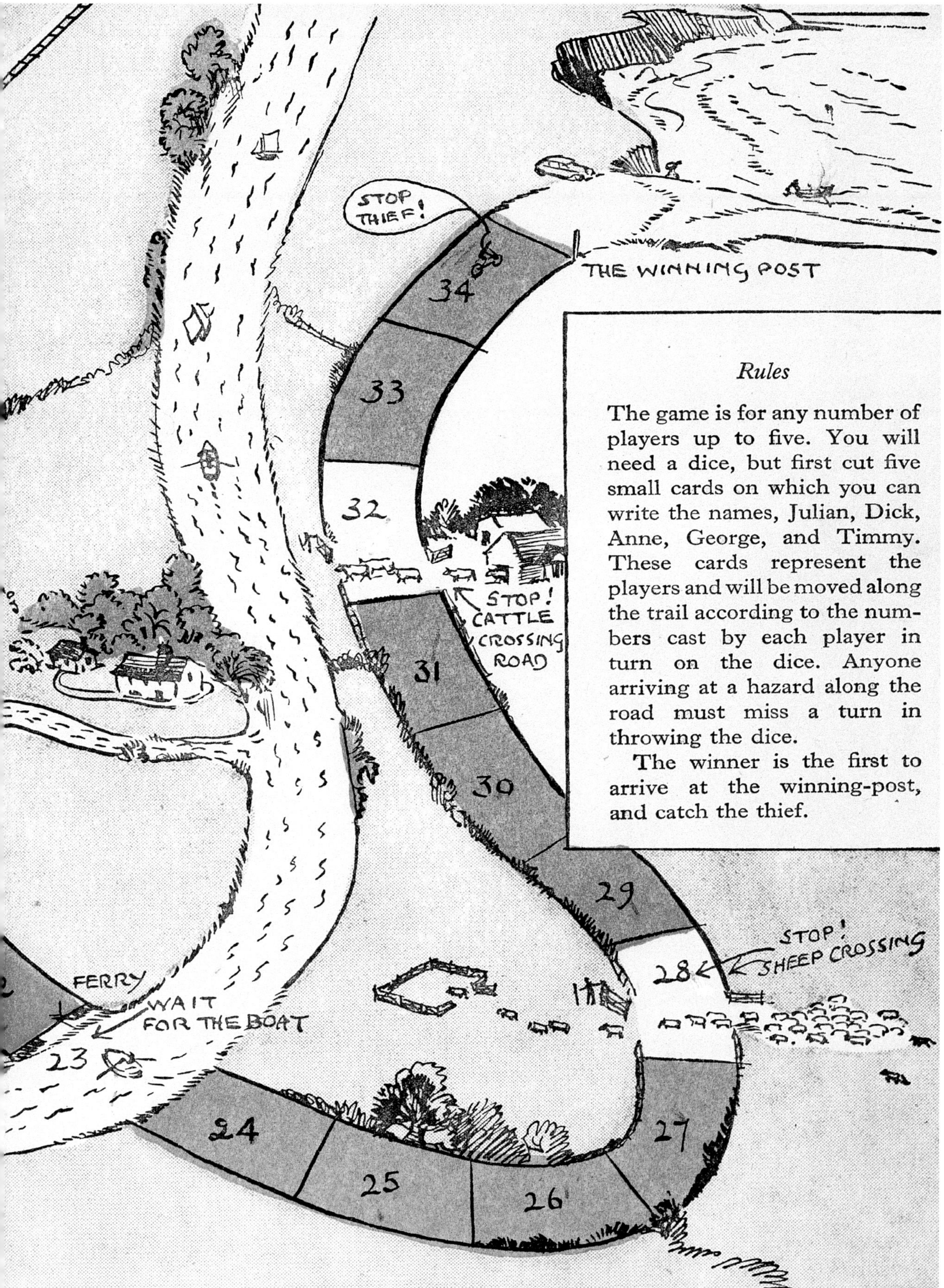

STOP THIEF!

34

33

32

31

30

29

THE WINNING POST

STOP! CATTLE CROSSING ROAD

STOP! SHEEP CROSSING

28

27

26

25

24

23

FERRY

WAIT FOR THE BOAT

Rules

The game is for any number of players up to five. You will need a dice, but first cut five small cards on which you can write the names, Julian, Dick, Anne, George, and Timmy. These cards represent the players and will be moved along the trail according to the numbers cast by each player in turn on the dice. Anyone arriving at a hazard along the road must miss a turn in throwing the dice.

The winner is the first to arrive at the winning-post, and catch the thief.

TO CATCH THE THIEVES

THE FAMOUS FIVE MUSICAL

There was a gap of 40 years between the first and second appearance of the Famous Five on stage. For four weeks over Easter, in March and April 1996, the King's Head Theatre, a small pub theatre in North London, staged a new version of the Famous Five as a daily matinee, written by John Hogg and Stephanie Crawford and directed by Dan Crawford. The story loosely followed *Five Go Adventuring Again*, with a bit tagged on to the beginning to show the initial meeting of George with her cousins. The big difference was that this version was a musical composed by Robert Dallas and it was set in 1938.

The four children were played by Peter England (Julian), Smedley Booth (Dick), Sarah Jones (George) and Olivia Hallinan (Anne), with David Powell Davies (Uncle Quentin) and Maggie Taylor (Aunt Fanny). It was very well received over the four week period and as a result it was decided that it should go on tour round the country in 1997, Enid Blyton's centenary year.

For a touring version they needed three teams of children and over the next few months, after the closing of the King's Head version, about 800 children were auditioned in various large cities. A week or so before Christmas, 24 children were invited to the final call back at the King's Head and from these they chose the final 12. Enid's elder daughter, Gillian Baverstock, who had acted as a consultant, helped with the final casting and mentioned that they ended up with four Julians, but sadly had to send one away as although he was a fine actor he didn't match up

to the other three in size. Olivia was the only survivor from the original version, but some of the adults reprised their roles including Quentin and Fanny (Olivia's mum in real life!). One of the teams had West End experience as three of them had been in the London Palladium production of *Oliver!*: Jon Lee (Julian), Ben McCosker (Dick) and Alison Hughes (George). Jon had played Oliver and Ben the Artful Dodger and Ben had also appeared in the Palace Theatre as Gavroche in *Les Miserables*. All three attended the Sylvia

The King's Head Theatre
115 Upper Street, Islington, London N1

Enid Blyton's

The Famous Five

LONDON ARTS BOARD

Young Theatre School in London. The fourth member of this team was Clare Fitton (Anne). She was much younger than the other three, but she also appeared in the touring version of *Oliver!* as Bets at the Manchester Opera House after the show had closed in London. Not surprisingly it was this experienced team that was in the version that was later released as a video and later still as a DVD. Whilst the musical was simply called *The Famous Five*, the video had *Smuggler's Gold* added on, presumably to make it sound more appealing!

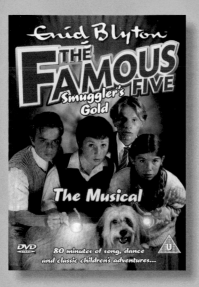

Intensive rehearsals began in early January in a Methodist Hall in Archway, north London. Things can't have been made easier by the fact that three of the children, Ben, Olivia and Vicky Taylor (another George), were also appearing in the Christmas production at the

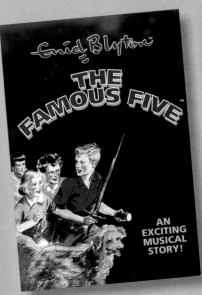

Apso cross, as the understudy! Both of these talented dogs had made numerous appearances on TV in both the UK and America and Emma had been awarded 'Top Trick Dog in the Country' in 1991.

The show opened in Basildon's Towngate Theatre on 30 January and was performed at 30 different locations round the country over the next seven months, finishing in Cardiff in the second week of August. In the advance publicity the producers had said that once the tour was over they hoped that the musical would transfer to the West End, but this was not to be. This was the exact opposite of the play that had been performed forty years previously, a West End show that had hoped to go on tour but didn't, followed by a touring musical version that sadly failed to find a berth in the West End.

King's Head Theatre of *Listen to the Wind*, which ran from 13 December to 19 January. The adult actors were added to the cast (not easy for them as they had to rehearse each scene with three teams of children) and last but by no means least was the introduction of Timmy to rehearsals.

Timmy was to be played by Sparkle, a two-year-old Lhasa Apso cross owned and trained by Janis McLeod, with Emma her mother, also a Lhasa

Enid Blyton™

THE FAMOUS FIVE™

THE CAST

(The parts of the children are played by three teams)

Red Team	
ANNE	Elizabeth Marsland
JULIAN	Lyndon Ogbourne
DICK	Matthew Johnson
GEORGE	Vicky Taylor

Blue Team	
ANNE	Olivia Hallinan
JULIAN	Gareth Derrick
DICK	Richard Power
GEORGE	Michelle Wright

Green Team	
ANNE	Clare Fitton
JULIAN	Jon Lee
DICK	Ben McCosker
GEORGE	Alison Hughes

UNCLE QUENTIN	David Powell Davies
AUNT FANNY	Maggie Taylor
MR ROLAND	Jason Webb
MR THOMAS	Mark Jardine
MR WILTON	Martin Head
GUARD/POLICEMAN	Graeme Braidwood
GUARD/POLICEMAN	Ian Connop

TIMMY THE DOG TRAINED BY
Janis McLeod

THE MUSICAL IS SET IN 1938

HAPPY CHRISTMAS, FIVE!

'Annual time' means Christmas is on its way, so here's a taster of a Christmas story that quickly turns into a mystery …

Christmas Eve at Kirrin Cottage – and the Five were all there together! They were up in the boys' bedroom, wrapping Christmas presents in bright paper. Timmy was very excited, and nosed about the room, his long tail wagging in delight.

'Don't keep slapping my legs with your tail, Tim,' said Anne. 'Look out, George, he's getting tangled up with your ball of string!'

'Don't look round, Anne, I'm wrapping up your present,' said Dick. 'There'll be a lot to give out this Christmas, with all of us here – and everyone giving everyone else something!'

'I've a B-O-N-E for Timmy,' said Anne, 'but it's downstairs in the larder. I was afraid he'd sniff it out up here.'

'Woof,' said Timmy, slapping his tail against Anne's legs again. 'He knows perfectly well that B-O-N-E spells bone,' said Julian. 'Now you've made him sniff all about *my* parcels! Timmy – go downstairs, please!'

'Oh no – he does so love Christmas time, and helping us to wrap up parcels,' said George. 'Sit, Timmy. SIT, I say. That's the third time you've knocked down my pile of presents.'

Downstairs, her father and mother were wrapping up parcels, too. They seemed to have as many as the four cousins upstairs! Mrs Kirrin looked at the pile of packages on the table.

'Far too many to go on the tree!' she said. 'We'd better put all our parcels and the children's too into a sack, Quentin. We can stand the sack at the bottom of the tree, and you can be Father Christmas and hand them out tomorrow morning.'

'I am NOT going to be Father Christmas,' said

Mr Kirrin. 'All this nonsense at Christmas time! Bits of paper everywhere – parcels to undo – Timmy barking his head off. Listen to him now! I'll go mad! He's to go to his kennel.'

'No, no, Quentin – don't upset George on Christmas Eve,' said Mrs Kirrin. 'Look – you go and sit down quietly in your study and read the paper. *I'll* finish the parcels. But you MUST be good and hand them out to the children tomorrow morning – yes, and hand Timmy's to him too.'

Supper-time came all too soon that night. When the bell rang to tell the Five that the meal was ready, they groaned.

'Have to finish afterwards,' said Dick, looking round at the mess of parcels, paper, string, ribbon and labels. 'Supper, Timmy, supper!'

Timmy shot downstairs at top speed, bumping heavily into Mr Kirrin, who was just coming out of his study. Timmy gave him a quick lick of apology, and ran into the dining room, putting his front feet on the table to see what was there.

'Down, Timmy – what manners!' said Julian.

'Hello, Uncle Quentin – done up all your parcels yet?'

His uncle grunted. Aunt Fanny laughed. 'He's going to be Father Christmas tomorrow morning and hand out all the presents,' she said. 'Don't scowl like that, Quentin dear – you look just like George when I tell her to fetch something!'

'I do NOT scowl,' said George, scowling immediately, of course. Everyone roared at her, and she had to smile.

'Christmas Day tomorrow,' said Anne happily. 'Aunt Fanny, it's lovely of you to have us all here for Christmas. We'll never finish opening our parcels tomorrow morning! I've got at least one for everybody, and so has everyone else.'

'A nice little bit of arithmetic,' said Julian. 'That means we've about forty or more presents to undo – counting in those for Joanna and Timmy.'

'What a waste of time!' That remark came from Uncle Quentin, of course!

'It's a good thing you're not as horrible as you pretend to be, Dad,' said George, and grinned at him. 'You always look so fierce – and yet I bet you've been round the shops buying all kinds of things. Hasn't he, Mum? I bet he's bought Timmy something, too.'

'Stop saying "I bet",' said her father. 'And don't

27

put ideas in Timmy's head. Why on earth should I go shopping for *him*?'

'Woof!' said Timmy, from under the table, delighted to hear his name. He wagged his tail violently and Mr Kirrin leapt to his feet with a yell.

'Take that dog out! Slapping me with his tail like that! Why can't he have a short tail? I'll . . .'

'Sit down, Quentin,' said his wife. 'Timmy, come out. Sit over there. Now – let's change the subject!'

The four cousins looked at one another and grinned. It was lovely to be at Kirrin Cottage again, with dear kind Aunt Fanny, and quick-tempered Uncle Quentin. He was now beaming round at them, offering them a second helping.

'No thanks,' said Dick. 'I'm saving up for the pudding. I spotted it in the larder – scrumptious!'

After supper they finished their parcels, and brought them all down to the sitting room. The tree was there, looking very cheerful, although the candles on it were not yet lighted. It was hung with tinsel and little sparkling ornaments, and had at the top the fairy doll that had been on every Christmas tree since George was little.

The parcels were put into a big sack, and this was set at the foot of the tree, ready for the morning. Timmy immediately went to sniff at it, from top to bottom.

'He can smell his Christmas bone,' said Anne. 'Timmy, come away. I won't have you guessing my present!'

Later they played games, and Timmy joined in. He was so excited that he began to bark, and Uncle Quentin stormed out of his study at once, and appeared in the sitting room.

'George! I've told you before I won't have Timmy barking in the house. Yes, I know it's Christmas Eve, but I can't STAND that barking. Why must he have such a loud one? It's enough to deafen me. I'll turn him out. He can go to his kennel!'

'Oh *no*, Dad – not on Christmas Eve!' said George, horrified. 'Timmy, go and lie down – and BE QUIET!'

'He's to go out to his kennel,' said her father.

'That's my last word. Out, Timmy, OUT!'

So out poor Timmy had to go, his tail well down. He felt puzzled. The children had been shouting, hadn't they? It was their way of barking. Well, why couldn't *he* shout in *his* own way, which was barking?

George was cross, and Anne was almost in tears. Poor Timmy – to be sent out to his kennel on Christmas Eve! She went to comfort George, and was surprised to see that she wasn't looking upset.

'Don't worry, Anne – I'll fetch him in when we go to bed and he can sleep in our room as usual,' she said.

'You can't do that!' said Anne. 'Uncle Quentin would be *furious* if he discovered him there.'

'He won't,' said George. 'It's no good, Anne

– I'm going to have Timmy with me tonight, although I KNOW I shouldn't. I couldn't bear not to. I'll own up to Dad tomorrow.'

So, when the household was safely in bed, George crept downstairs to fetch Timmy from his kennel. He whined softly in joy and wagged his big tail.

'Be quiet now,' whispered George, and took him upstairs – completely forgetting to lock the kitchen door! Timmy settled down on the rug beside her bed, very happy, and soon Anne and George were fast asleep in their beds, while the two boys slept soundly in their room nearby.

What disturbs Timmy's sleep? Read the rest of the story to find out ...

WHAT'S WRONG?

Pepys Famous Five Card Games

Eileen Soper who had made nine deliberate errors on each picture. The purpose of the game was simply to find as many errors as you could in a fixed time – the rules suggested ten minutes for each picture. The cards in Series 1 were: *No. 1. The Famous Five as Detectives*, *No. 2. The Famous Five at Kirrin Cottage* and *No. 3. The Famous Five at the Circus Camp*. In Series 2 the pictures were, *No. 1. The Five visit the Gypsies*, *No. 2. The Five Go on Holiday* and *No. 3. The Five in Camp.*

On the next two pages you will see some of the original Eileen Soper illustrations from the two games and also a larger picture of *The Five in Camp* for you to have a go at yourself. There are nine deliberate errors in the picture, some of which aren't immediately obvious. See how many you are able to find. The solutions are below and on page 64.

Pepys, owned by Castell Brothers, produced a range of card games for children in the 1940s and 50s. In 1950 they brought out *The Faraway Tree Card Game*, which was their first game to be based on an Enid Blyton series. This sold well and in 1951 they followed this with *The Famous Five Card Game* which was based on four of the Famous Five books (*Treasure Island*, *Smuggler's Top*, *Caravan* and *Trouble*) and the cards were all illustrated by Eileen Soper. This also sold well and encouraged Pepys to add a Famous Five game to their range.

Their party games all came in uniformly designed boxes and whilst most were produced for adults, a few were specially designed for children. All the games were different and the Famous Five one came with the title *What's Wrong?* Once again the Famous Five proved popular and a couple of years later they issued a Series 2 edition, one of only two party games for children to have a second version released, the other being *Dan Dare* (a treasure hunt).

The game was designed for two to twelve children and each box came with twelve large cards and a set of rules, which also listed the solutions. There were four cards of each of three designs and they were specially illustrated by

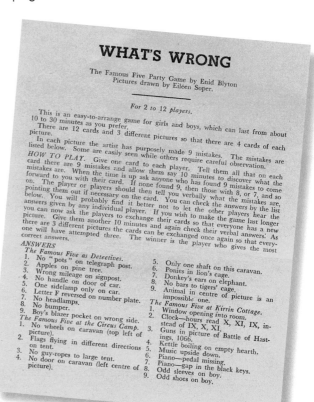

WHAT'S WRONG

The Famous Five Party Game by Enid Blyton
Pictures drawn by Eileen Soper.

For 2 to 12 players.

This is an easy-to-arrange game for girls and boys, which can last from about 10 to 30 minutes as you prefer.

There are 12 cards and 3 different pictures so that there are 4 cards of each picture.

In each picture the artist has purposely made 9 mistakes. The mistakes are listed below. Some are easily seen while others require careful observation.

HOW TO PLAY. Give one card to each player. Tell them all that on each card there are 9 mistakes and allow them say 10 minutes to discover what the mistakes are. When the time is up ask anyone who has found 9 mistakes to come forward to you with their card. If none found 9, then those with 8, or 7, and so on. The player or players should then tell you verbally what the mistakes are, pointing them out if necessary on the card. You can check the answers by the list below. You will probably find it better not to let the other players hear the answers given by any individual player. If you wish to make the game last longer you can now ask the players to exchange their cards so that everyone has a new picture. Give them another 10 minutes and again check their verbal answers. As there are 3 different pictures the cards can be exchanged once again so that every one will have attempted three. The winner is the player who gives the most correct answers.

ANSWERS

The Famous Five as Detectives.
1. No "pots" on telegraph post.
2. Apples on pine tree.
3. Wrong mileage on signpost.
4. No handle on door of car.
5. One sidelamp only on car.
6. Letter F reversed on number plate.
7. No headlamps.
8. No bumper.
9. Boy's blazer pocket on wrong side.
The Famous Five at the Circus Camp.
1. No wheels on caravan (top left of picture).
2. Flags flying in different directions on tent.
3. No guy-ropes to large tent.
4. No door on caravan (left centre of picture).

5. Only one shaft on this caravan.
6. Ponies in lion's cage.
7. Donkey's ears on elephant.
8. No bars to tigers' cage.
9. Animal in centre of picture is an impossible one.
The Famous Five at Kirrin Cottage.
1. Window opening into room.
2. Clock—hours read X, XI, IX, instead of IX, X, XI.
3. Guns in picture of Battle of Hastings, 1066.
4. Kettle boiling on empty hearth.
5. Music upside down.
6. Piano—pedal missing.
7. Piano—gap in the black keys.
8. Odd sleeves on boy.
9. Odd shoes on boy.

WHAT'S WRONG? The Five in Camp No. 3

A TOUR ROUND KIRRIN ISLAND

You may think you know your way around Kirrin – but do you? Come on a tour of the Cottage, Island, Castle, the common and other places around the village where we would all love to live!

Beckton

A fairly large town with a cinema and a town hall several miles away from Kirrin. It can be reached by road but, as it is several miles from Kirrin, the Five usually travel there by train.

Kirrin Hill

A hill close to Kirrin Cottage where the Five sometimes go to have a picnic.

Kirrin Station

The Five usually arrive at Kirrin by train where they are met by Aunt Fanny in the pony and trap. Kirrin Station is a short distance inland from Kirrin Cottage. The station can be reached by walking across the moors at the back of the cottage. In *Five Run Away Together* the Five leave a railway timetable open and then set out across the moor to the back of the cottage in order to fool the Stick family into thinking that they are going away by train.

Coastguard Cottage

Standing on the cliffs overlooking Kirrin Bay and Kirrin Island is the little whitewashed coastguard cottage where the coastguard, 'a red faced, barrel-shaped man, fond of joking and with an enormous voice,' lives. Like almost everyone who lives in Kirrin, the coastguard knows and likes the Five and whenever they call at his cottage he lets the children use his large, powerful telescope to look out to sea and view Kirrin Island. This was particularly useful when Uncle Quentin was staying on the Island conducting one of his experiments and George wanted to use the telescope to see Timmy, who was staying with him on the island (*Five On Kirrin Island Again*). The coastguard will often be found in his large shed where he makes wooden toys to sell. Two other cottages stand beside the coastguard cottage and one of these at least is let out to holidaymakers. The coastguard cottage can be reached by either a cliff path from Kirrin Cottage or along the road that runs from the back of the cliff to Kirrin Village.

Kirrin Castle

The castle, built of big, white stones, stands on a low hill in the centre of Kirrin Island. It has two towers, one of which is in total ruins and the other in which jackdaws nest. A strong wall once surrounded the castle but it but this has long since crumbled away. The entrance is through a broken archway and down a flight of uneven steps into the castle yard. The stone slabs that once paved the yard are now broken and covered in sand, blown in from the shore. Where slabs are missing blackberry and gorse bushes have grown up.

When the Five first went to the Island together, looking for the lost gold ingots, they cleared many of the bushes from the castle yard while searching for an entrance to the dungeons. It was Anne who eventually found the stone slab with the iron ring in it that covered the entrance they sought.

The castle dungeons, where long ago prisoners were kept, are deep underground and are cut into the solid rock. It is dark and damp in the dungeons and noises echo round, making it very eerie. A passage runs under the seabed from the dungeons to the old quarry on Kirrin Common.

The old castle well is also in the yard. This was inadvertently discovered by Timmy when he chased a rabbit down a hole and found himself calling through space! Luckily he landed on a slab of stone that had fallen and jammed itself partway down the well-shaft. The well-shaft runs through the dungeons where there is a small opening. This was used by the Five to escape from the dungeons when they were imprisoned there in *Five On A Treasure Island*.

The castle is now in ruins and only one room,

jutting out from what had once been the wall of the castle, remains nearly complete. It was in this room, with its two slit windows and recess where a fireplace had once been, that the Five camped in their first adventure and where later, in *Five On Kirrin Island Again*, George discovered the entrance to undersea caves and a passage that led under the sea-bed to the mainland.

Kirrin Common

Behind Kirrin Cottage stretches the common, sometimes called the moor. Some areas are lonely and rarely visited and it is to one of these parts that the Five go camping in *Five On a Secret Trail*. They travel along Carters Lane and then take one of the winding footpaths over the common. Up a hill, then down into a little copse, brings them close to a ruined cottage that is covered with rambling rose. Near the building is a good spot to camp, with a spring once used by the inhabitants of the cottage, which runs through an age-old channel made of white stone. Close to the spring the Five discover the entrance to a secret passage. Near the ruin is a pool where the children can swim, and the site of an ancient Roman Camp.

Kirrin Cottage

Kirrin Cottage stands on a low cliff overlooking Kirrin Bay with an easy path leading down to the beach. It is not really a cottage but quite a large old house, built about 300 years ago. A crazy paving path leads up to the porch and the front door. The walls are of white stone but much of the wall is covered with climbing roses and ivy. The ivy is so thick in places that in one adventure Jo climbed up the ivy and looked in at the window of the girls' room.

Inside the cottage is a sitting room, a dining room and a large kitchen where Joanna, the cook, will usually be found baking or preparing a meal. Next to the kitchen is a scullery. At the back of the house, overlooking the garden, is Uncle Quentin's study where he keeps his important papers and carries out his experiments. The Five are rarely allowed in this room with its panelled walls and stone floor but one winter's night, when Timmy had been banished outside to live in a kennel, George smuggled him into the study and while there discovered the entrance to the Secret Way.

Upstairs the boys share a room with a slanting ceiling and a window that overlooks Kirrin Bay and Kirrin Island. George and Anne share a room with two windows. One of these has a view over the moor at the back of the house, while the other 'looked sideways at the sea'. In Aunt Fanny's room is a large store-cupboard packed with tinned food in case the cottage is snowed up in winter, as sometimes happens. At the very top of the house is the attic bedroom where Joanna, the cook, sleeps.

In spring, the garden is ablaze with colourful flowers: primroses, wallflowers and daffodils. There is a garden shed with two wheelbarrows, a summerhouse, an outhouse for the chickens and somewhere to keep the pony and trap. There are fruit trees, and a vegetable garden where tomatoes are grown. A giant Ash tree once stood close to the cottage but during a storm (*Five Go To Smuggler's Top*) it was pulled up by its roots and came crashing down on the house destroying the attic, the girls' bedroom and most of the roof.

Kirrin Farmhouse

If the Five are staying at Kirrin Cottage and the sea is too rough for them to row across to Kirrin Island they will often visit Kirrin Farmhouse to chat with Mr and Mrs Sanders and explore the

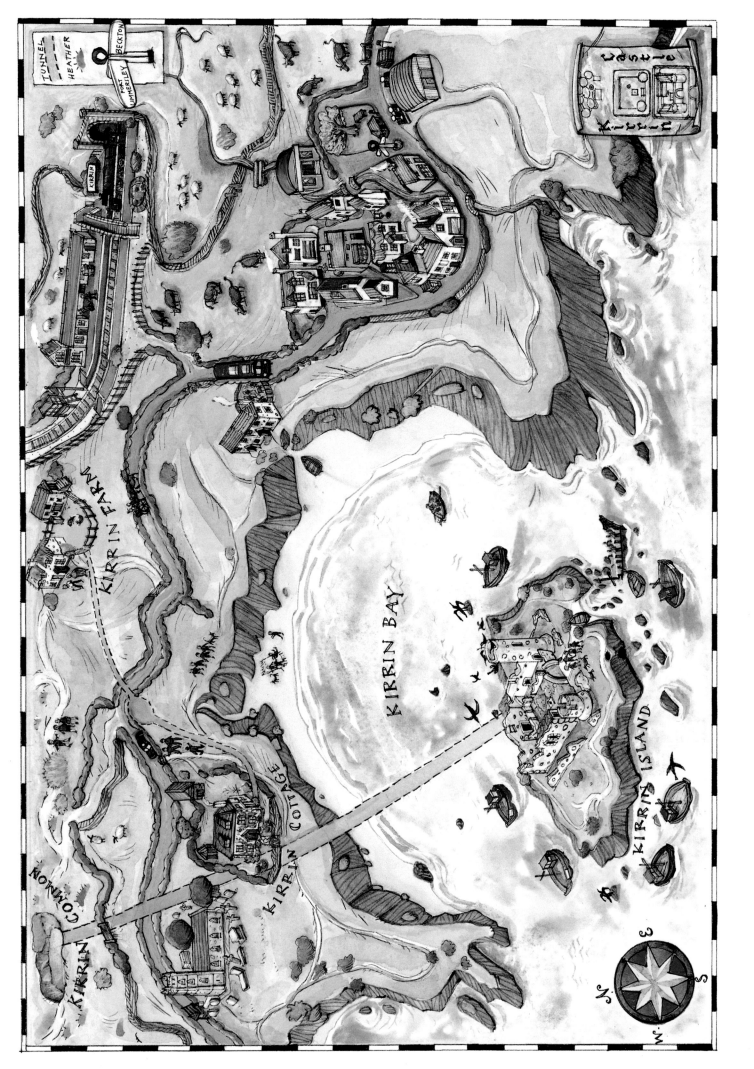

secret nooks and crannies of the old building. It's a pleasant walk to the farm, down the lane then along the track that leads across the common behind Kirrin Cottage. The farmhouse is visible from some distance as it stands on a low hill and the white stone of which it is built gleams in the sunlight. If it is spring or summer the children will probably see some of the farm's sheep grazing in the fields, while Timmy will be on the lookout for the farm's tabby cat. As the Five approach the farmhouse Ben and Rikky, the two farm dogs, will bark to announce their arrival.

Inside the big, north-facing farmhouse kitchen there is always a warm welcome from Mrs Sanders, the farmer's wife. The farm is very old, built in the days when it was sometimes important to be able to hide or escape from enemies, and there are all sorts of hidden cupboards, sliding panels and secret passages for the Five to explore. All the downstairs rooms have stone floors and in the hall, close to the majestic grandfather clock, is a secret sliding panel that opens when the top corner is pressed. Behind the panel is a narrow recess, deep enough to get an arm in but too small even for Anne to stand in. Mrs Sanders grumbles that every time she dusts she has to be careful or the panel shoots open. In a nook in the wall behind the panel Dick discovered an old book, and Julian, whose longer arm was able to reach in further, found an old tobacco pouch containing the plan of how to find the entrance to the Secret Way. Another hidey-hole can be found in the fireplace where a stone can be pulled up revealing a hole big enough to hide a small box.

Upstairs in one of the bedrooms is a cupboard with a sliding back leading to a space big enough for a man to stand hidden. What had been forgotten over the years was that beyond this is another secret door – it took the Famous Five to rediscover it!

Kirrin Island

Nestling in the bay is Kirrin Island, a small, rock-bound island that has been in George's mother's family for generations. In the centre of the island is Kirrin Castle. Deep water and sharp rocks surround the island and only an experienced oarsman can steer a boat through these dangers to the little natural harbour; a smooth inlet of water running up to a stretch of sand sheltered between high rocks on the east side of the island. In winter, when the sea is rough, it is impossible to land on the island. Because of the rocks and strong currents it is impossible to swim out to the island.

Kirrin Island is full of wild flowers and large gorse bushes and is the home to gulls, cormorants, jackdaws and countless rabbits. Since so few people visit the island the rabbits are very tame and show little fear of people when they approach. Timmy finds it almost impossible not to chase the rabbits but he knows that this is the one rule that George is *very* strict about. Rabbits are the only things that Timmy and George disagree on!

During *Five On Kirrin Island Again*, Uncle Quentin stayed on Kirrin Island to conduct some important experiments. He built a tall tower made of smooth, shiny material that fitted together in sections and had a narrow spiral staircase leading up to a little glass room at the top. Wires ran right through the glass and when he conducted an experiment the wires waved and lit up.

As far as George knows there is only one cave on Kirrin Island. This was discovered on the seaward side of the island by Dick as the Five made their way back to the beach after clambering over a rocky part of the shore to look at the old wreck. Tall rocks almost completely hide the cave entrance. Inside it is perfectly dry as the sea only reaches it during the very worst winter storms. The floor is covered with fine white sand and along one side runs a ledge. In the roof of the cave is an opening that comes out onto the cliff-top. This is hard to find amongst the heather and brambles which criss-crossed it keeping it well hidden. In *Five Run Away Together* the Five camped out in the cave – and even captured a prisoner who fell down the hole in the roof!

Kirrin Village

Kirrin is a large, thriving seaside village with many shops. These include: an ironmonger's, a baker's, a dairy, a hairdresser's, a draper's, a butcher's, a chemist's and a general store. The village has a large hotel (the Rollins) and a garage where Jim, a boy known to the Five, works. In *Five Fall Into Adventure* we are told that it even has a cinema.

There is a railway station at Kirrin with trains running to the nearby villages of Seagreen Halt and Beckton. A bus runs down the lane in front of Kirrin Cottage.

There are lovely cliff-top walks from the village offering breathtaking views across Kirrin Bay and over to Kirrin Island. The area inland from Kirrin is fairly hilly with Kirrin Hill close by and Rilling Hill a little further away. A winding lane from the village leads to Windy Cove.

The Old Wreck

For many, many years the old wreck lay in deep water on the far side of Kirrin Island. It was a tall sailing ship that once belonged to Henry John Kirrin, George's great, great, great, grandfather. While he was using it to transport gold bars back to Kirrin Bay it was sunk in a fierce storm. During *Five On a Treasure Island* another storm dragged the wreck up from the sea-bed and set it down on the jagged rocks that surround the island. The Five are able to explore the old, shellfish-encrusted wreck where they make exciting discoveries. Later the rough winter seas moved the wreck onto rocks closer to Kirrin Island where, at low tide, it can be reached by clambering over the rocks from the shore.

Port Limmersley

The next place along the coast from Kirrin mentioned in *Five Fall Into Adventure*. It is here that Red Tower has his clifftop hide-out complete with a helicopter for a quick get-away. The coast between Kirrin and Port Limmersley is very desolate.

The Quarry

About a quarter of a mile across the moors (sometimes called the common), behind Kirrin Cottage, is the old quarry. In the past stone was extracted from it but now it is deserted and with no footpaths close by, few people visit it. It is shaped like a huge, rough bowl with steep sides. Small bushes, grass and plants grow down its sides and in the spring it is bright with primroses and violets. The Five sometimes go to the quarry searching for flint arrow-heads and enjoy a picnic there sheltered from the wind.

Seagreen

A tiny village between Kirrin and Beckton. There is a small railway station there and a few cottages. It is in one of these cottages that a valuable Pekinese dog, stolen from the dog show in **Beckton**, is being hidden in the short story entitled *Five and a Half-Term Adventure*.

Uncle Quentin's Tower

For one of his scientific investigations, Quentin Kirrin needed a place where he had water all around him. He took all of his equipment to Kirrin Island and had a strange tower built in the castle yard. It looked rather like a lighthouse but, instead of being built of brick, it was made in sections from some smooth, shiny material, that Julian guessed was a kind of plastic. The sections fitted together to form the tower and at the top was a room with walls of thick glass. A narrow spiral staircase led up to the room. Wires ran right through the glass and their free ends waved and glittered in the wind. When Quentin was experimenting the wires were activated by some secret power and the wires lit up. Quentin Kirrin's experiments here were very important for he was working on a new fuel that would replace coal, coke and oil.

ISLAND OF DANGER

The sea between Kirrin Bay and Kirrin Island is full of dangerous, jagged rocks. George is the only person who knows the way through – but she's stranded on the island. Can you guide Julian and the others safely to her?

A LADDER TO A BADDIE!

Look at the starting word and climb down the rungs of the ladder, changing one letter each time to create a new word on every rung. At the bottom of the ladder, you will come to a Blyton 'baddie'. The first is the mysterious servant Block from *Five Go to Smuggler's Top*, the second is the thuggish bodyguard Rooky from *Five Get Into Trouble*, and the third is the clever and calculating magician Wooh (Mr Wooh) from *Five Are Together Again*. Use the clues to help you find the word on each rung. If you complete all the words on a ladder, you can congratulate yourself on having caught the 'baddie'!

GRAND
- - - - - - - - -   A particular make; an identifying mark
- - - - - - - - -   Not very tasty
- - - - - - - - -   Empty
- - - - - - - - -   The colour of the night sky

BLOCK

LACES
- - - - - - - - -   Is without; is deficient in
- - - - - - - - -   Turns a key to secure something
- - - - - - - - -   Large stones
- - - - - - - - -   Big, black birds

ROOKY

PULL
- - - - - - - - -   Survey
- - - - - - - - -   A small area of water, sometimes used for swimming
- - - - - - - - -   We get this from sheep

WOOH

FIVE GET INTO A FIX
FIND-A-WORD

The seventeenth Famous Five novel takes place in a cold and snowy winter. The words hidden in this puzzle – forwards, backwards, or diagonally – will give you a flavour of some of the characters and events of the book.

```
S G W O N S S L C T O
T E F A N Y H A O C L
J R R E D N U T C H D
E M O N N E D E O R T
N C A F A L D M A I O
K O I G G G E N K S W
I R L L G L R E P T E
N O Y T O A E O H M R
S T H H B P G O M A S
I C T E O F M L E S N
D O R U T A T A E R T
P D T W S Y R U J N I
```

AILY	GLENYS	POLICE
BARNARD	INJURY	POTHOLE
CHRISTMAS	JENKINS	SHUDDER
COCOA	KEEP OUT	SNOW
DOCTOR	MAGGA GLEN	THOMAS
FANY	METAL	TOBOGGAN
FORT	MORGAN	TREAT
GERM	OLD TOWERS	UNDER

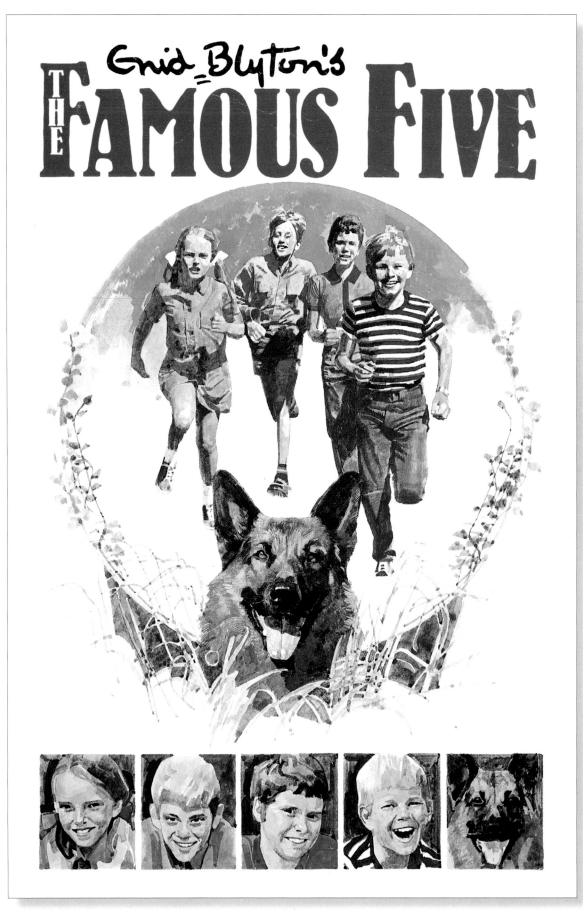

This is the cover of the American video of the 1970 Danish film, *Five Get Into Trouble*, which was dubbed into English (by Darrell Waters, who owned the Blyton Estate). It was released in America, but never in the UK.

FIVE ON KIRRIN ISLAND AGAIN

Here's an extract from a comic strip based on the sixth adventure in the series. Enid took the Five back to Kirrin Island because she intended it to be the last in the series – so there are plenty of references to *Five On a Treasure Island*. The end of the original book sounds quite final: 'Now we must say good-bye to the Five, and to Kirrin Island too. Good-bye, Julian, Dick, George, Anne – and Timmy. But only Timmy hears our good-bye, for he has such sharp ears. "Woof! Good-bye!" Luckily, Enid's many fans wrote to her, demanding new stories.

HIDDEN MESSAGES

In *Five Go Adventuring Again*, the mysterious clues, written in Latin on the piece of linen, kept the Five guessing until Mr Roland discovered that they were directions for finding the entrance to the Secret Way. Codes are vital ways of exchanging important – and secret – information. You can have fun swapping secret codes amongst your friends. Here are a few examples to set you off. When you have mastered them, why not try to invent a code of your own?

Here's a very simple code to start with – using numbers for letters of the alphabet. 1 for A, 2 for B, 3 for C, and so on. If you wanted to write THE FAMOUS FIVE you would use the following numbers: 20 8 5 6 1 13 15 21 19 6 9 22 5. The snag with this code, of course, is your secret

message would very soon be solved. To make it more difficult, start numbering further down the alphabet. Instead of A being number 1, for example, make the letter H number 1, I 2, J 3, K 4 and so on, finishing up with G being numbered 26.

Here's another number/letter code. Divide a square into 25 smaller squares and put one letter of the alphabet into each box. As there are 26 letters, you will have to put two letters in one of the boxes. We'll put I and J in the same box (see below). This is how the code works. Suppose you want the letter H. It's in row 2, column 3 – so the number for H is 23. If you wanted S, it's in row 4, column 3 – so the number for S is 43.

	1	2	3	4	5
1	A	B	C	D	E
2	F	G	H	IJ	K
3	L	M	N	O	P
4	Q	R	S	T	U
5	V	W	X	Y	Z

FIVE GO DOWN TO THE SEA WORD CROSS

Who is flashing lights from the old tower on wild and stormy nights – and why? The twelfth book in the series features some of Blyton's most memorable characters and a truly puzzling mystery.

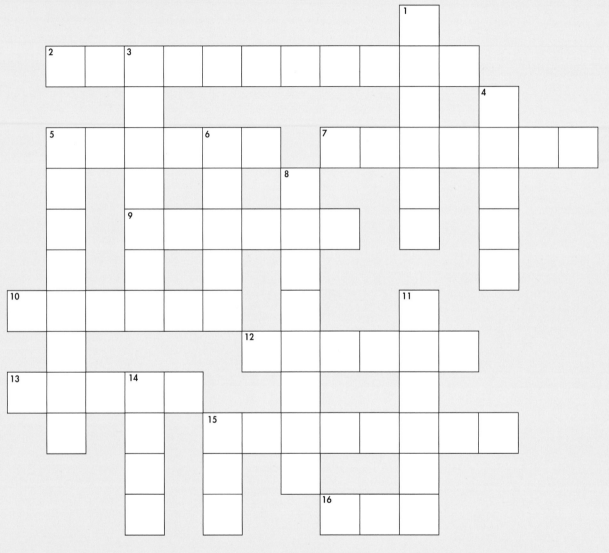

ACROSS

2. Early in the book, the boy Yan keeps puzzling the Five. Time and again, it seems he's _____. What?

5. Where do you end up if you walk across the fields?

7. By what name are the strolling players known?

9. Who is the 'grim-faced man' supervising the moving of bales?

10. Yan is seldom given these, but loves them!

12 and 4 down. Two of the dogs in the novel.

13. Complete the sentence. 'The lane ran down between two high rocky _____ and in front of them was a cove.'

15. What word does Anne use to describe Mr Penruthan?

16. Complete the name: Wreckers _____ .

DOWN

1. Timmy follows a trail of oil drips, which ends here.

3. This word means to transport goods without permission.

4. See 12 across.

5. The county in which this story is set.

6. A good place for hiding.

8. John, the porter's surname.

11. A synonym for dirty which describes Yan.

14. What sort of property is Tremannon?

15. One of the men who dresses up as Clopper.

UP ON THE MOORS

An extract from *Five Go Off to Camp . . .*

THE FAMOUS FIVE IN AMERICA

The only Enid Blyton book that ever won a prize was *Mystery Island* in 1947. If this title should seem unfamiliar to Blyton fans it is because the prize was awarded in America, by the Boys' Club of America for one of the six most popular books of that year and it was a retitled version of *The Island of Adventure*. It seems ironic that one of the bestselling children's authors of the 20th century should get her only award in what, for her, was fairly infertile territory. Odder still that the book had originally been published in America in 1945, so it must have been the 3rd edition that caught the eye of the judges!

It was possibly as a result of this success that a New York publisher, Thomas Y Crowell, decided to try another Enid Blyton series and in 1950 they published *Five On a Treasure Island*. The text stuck to the original book apart from one or two very minor alterations to suit American children, such as 'summer holidays' turned into 'summer vacation'. The cover was illustrated by Vera Neville, who also provided 26 internal illustrations. Thomas Y Crowell followed this in 1951 by publishing

Five Go Adventuring Again, which was also illustrated by Vera Neville, but possibly the books had disappointing sales as at this point the publisher decided to do no further books.

It wasn't until the following decade that another publisher tried their luck with the Famous Five. Chicago publishers Reilly & Lee published the next two books in the series, *Five Run Away Together* and *Five Go to Smuggler's Top*, both in 1960. This time the covers were illustrated by an uncredited artist, but the books both had 24 of Eileen Soper's original 32 illustrations. Another two books from Reilly & Lee came out in 1961, but

this time they jumped to *Five Go Down to the Sea* and *Five Go to Mystery Moor*. These books credited the cover illustrator as Frank Aloise (who was probably also the illustrator for the

more 'snappy' titles. 'Go Adventuring Again' turned into *Five Find a Secret Way*, 'Run Away Together' into *Five Run Away to Danger*, 'On Kirrin Island Again' into *Five Guard a Hidden Discovery*, 'Go Off to Camp' into *Five on the Trail of a Spook Train* and 'Get Into Trouble' into *Five Caught in a Treacherous Plot*. These books are long out of print.

Perhaps the Famous Five will one day be published in America again?

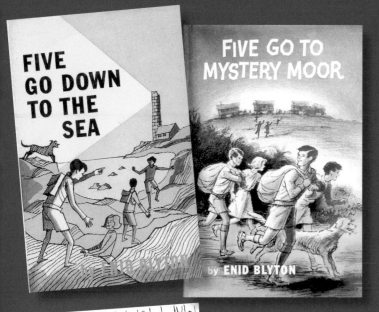

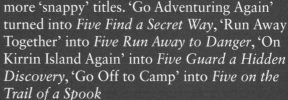

covers of the first two books), and he also replaced Eileen Soper for the internal artwork with eight full-page illustrations. The rear flap had this to say, 'Frank Aloise is a New York artist on the art staff of NBC. His decorative illustration of children's books has been widely praised.' At this point Reilly and Lee also decided to call it a day.

A further 11 years passed before the Famous Five again surfaced in America. In 1972 Atheneum (an American imprint of Macmillan) started releasing several Famous Five titles first as hardbacks and then as paperbacks in their Aladdin Series. This time they used the Betty Maxey illustrations from the UK Knight editions. There was one main difference as Atheneum decided that five of the books needed slightly

THE FIENDISH FAMOUS FIVE QUIZ

How well do you know the Famous Five? Here are 20 brain-teasing questions to test your knowledge. On your mark, get set, go!

1. In *Five On a Treasure Island*, only one of the villains who goes to Kirrin Island to try and steal the gold ingots in the Five's first adventure is named. What is his name?

2. Why was Uncle Quentin going to Smuggler's Top in the book that shares that title?

3. What does the Kirrin coastguard do for a hobby? (See *Five On Kirrin Island Again*.)

4. While on the moor in *Five On A Hike Together*, the Five go through Coney Copse and Julian explains that 'coney' is a country word for something with which they are all very familiar – particularly Timmy! What does it mean?

5. Who is the first of the Five to travel through the secret passage that runs under the sea from Kirrin Island to the mainland? (See *Five Go Off In A Caravan*.)

6. Name the farm on which the Five are staying in *Five Go Down to the Sea*?

7. In *Five Go Off to Camp*, what is the name of the pigling owned by Benny at Billycock Farm?

8. At the end of *Five On a Hike Together* how do the children get back to their schools? (See *Five On A Hike Together*)?

9. What does Berta Wright, the little American girl in *Five Have Plenty Of Fun* call her father?

10. What is the name of the wild little girl who roams the Welsh mountainside with her pet lamb and dog in *Five Get Into A Fix*?

11. Who works on the golf course and tells the Five the story of Whispering Island? (See *Five Have a Mystery To Solve*)?

12. Throughout *Five Go to Mystery Moor* we hear of patrins. What are these?

13. *In Five Run Away Together* where do the Five camp on Kirrin Island?

14. How does Jo get into the tower room to rescue George in *Five in a Caravan*?

15. Old Lady is the elephant at Mr Gorgio's circus. What does she like to do when she is having a bath in the lake? (See *Five Go Off in a Caravan*.)

16. What is the name of the lane that runs over Kirrin Common? (See *Five On a Secret Trail*.)

17. What is the name of the old blacksmith who explains to the children how Mystery Moor got its name (*Five Go to Mystery Moor*)?

18. Name the newspaper delivery boy with whom Dick changes places in *Five Fall Into Adventure*?

19. In the first book of the series, how is Dick's cheek injured when they are trying to open the dungeon door at Kirrin Castle?

20. What is the name of the small lake on the moor close to the ruined house named Two Trees where the Five go to search for hidden jewels in *Five on a Hike Together*?

FIVE GO ADVENTURING AGAIN

In this extract we meet Mr Roland – one of the least popular characters in the series. But he's not the only person the Five need to worry about . . .

55

58

CASTLES AND OTHER BUILDINGS

Demon's Rocks Lighthouse was built during the 1890s to prevent ships from being dragged onto the dangerous Demon's Rocks by the strong currents. Money for its construction was provided by a rich man whose daughter had been drowned in a ship wrecked on the Rocks. When a new, more powerful lighthouse was built at High Cliffs the old building became disused and was bought by Professor Hayling who later gave it to his son, Tinker.

The lighthouse is built well out on the rocks and at high tide can be reached only by boat from the stone jetty on the quay. When the tide is out, it is possible to wade across to it. Stone steps lead up from the rocks to the stout door, opened with a very large key, and inside an iron spiral-staircase leads up to the various rooms. First there is the store room and then the oil room where the oil to power the light was once kept. Next you will arrive at one of the few rooms with a window and this is now used as a bedroom. Continue up the staircase and you come to the living room. This has a higher roof than other rooms in the building. In it is a table, desk and chairs, as well as a paraffin stove for boiling water and frying food, and an oil lamp to provide light for the room. Over the little sink is a tank with a pipe leading from it to 'catch tank' fixed on the outside west wall of the lighthouse to catch rainwater.

At the top of the lighthouse is the lamp room where the great old oil lamp once shone out to warn ships. There are windows all round and a small door that leads out on to a gallery. Here a large bell once hung that would be rung during foggy weather to warn ships of the rocks. At the base of the lighthouse is a trapdoor with a ladder leading down into the foundations of the building. The foundations are built round a natural tunnel that has a passage at its base leading to the Wreckers' Cave. (In *Five Are Together Again* we are told that the lighthouse was later damaged in a storm.)

Big Hollow House is home to Tinker and Professor Hayling on the edge of Big Hollow Village, a bus ride away from Kirrin Village. The house has been owned by the family for hundreds of years and the Professor has an ancient parchment granting the family the rights to the field next to their garden, known as Cromwell's Corner, for all time. In the garden is a tall, slender tower with a rough stone wall partly covered in creepers, with 'curious tentacle-like rods sticking out at the top', where the Professor carries out his experiments and also stores many of his top secret papers.

Faynights Castle is several miles from the coast, set on top of a high hill. It originally had four towers but only one of these remains whole: the others are in a state of almost total ruin. The walls are over two metres thick and within some of them runs a secret passage.

The view from the castle is magnificent and sentries would have seen for miles around the surrounding countryside. There is a small village close to the castle and a number of caravans park in the nearby Faynights Field.

Finniston Castle is a small castle built in Norman times but burnt down by enemies in 1192. Over the years all the stones were removed from the site and people forgot the exact location of the castle. While digging into a rabbit hole on **Finniston Farm** Timmy and Snippet uncover the castle's midden (rubbish dump) and this gives the Five a clue to the whereabouts of the secret passage that was once supposed to run from the castle to the chapel.

Owl's Dene, named after the screech owls that inhabit its grounds, is the old Tudor mansion with tall chimneys situated on lonely Owl's Hill where Mr Perton and his gang, including the violent Rooky, plans crimes. The house has large, rambling grounds with a high wall all around it and wrought iron gates that are opened and closed by machinery operated from inside the house. The house is self-contained with its own cows, hens and ducks as well as a vegetable patch. There are, however, few comforts at Owl's Dene with no water, gas or electricity supplies. Julian, George, Anne, Timmy and Richard Kent go to Owl's Dene in search of Dick after he is mistakenly kidnapped. While attempting to free him they discover a secret room where escaped convicts are hidden. It's hidden behind a bookcase and is used to hide escaped convicts from the police. Julian discovers the room after following the sound of snoring made by Solomon Weston who was being hidden in the room.

A good way along the coast from Kirrin is **Smuggler's Top**, the home of Pierre and Marybelle Lenoir. It is old and mysterious and built on the top of Castaway Hill with one side on the very edge of the steep cliff that falls away to the marshes that surround the hill. On the east side of the house is a round tower that looks out across the marshes to the sea. Smuggler's Top, like many ancient buildings, has secret passages built within its walls and Pierre takes the Five through these passages to explore the tunnels and Catacombs that honeycomb Castaway Hill.

Close to the centre of the moor that lies between the boys' and girls' schools, Two Trees was once a grand house with a number of servants. The house is reached along a very narrow track and because of this fire engines could not reach it to put out a bad fire that left it a blackened ruin many years before. The two huge trees which gave the house its name, and which stood at each end of the house, were also burnt in the fire. Next to Two Trees is the small lake of **Gloomy Water** with a ruined boathouse nestling up a short backwater. When the Five go to Two Trees on their hike they camp in the underground room next to the cellars where the servants once had their quarters. While at Two Trees the Five run into two disreputable characters named **Dirty Dick** (**Taggart**) and **Maggie** (**Martin**) who are looking for stolen jewels hidden by a criminal named Nailer. The unpleasant pair are beaten to the jewels by the Five

and end up becoming stuck in Green Marshes, where they have to be rescued by the police.

On the Cornish coast close to Tremannon Farm is an old house with a tower once used by Wreckers. On dark and stormy nights the wreckers would set a light in the tower-room to lure ships on to the rocks in Tremannon Cove. The house, which can only be approached along a narrow overgrown lane that seems to the Five like a 'green tunnel', is now deserted and in a state of ruin. The massive old door that led to the tower has fallen and lies like a large slab on the floor. A spiral staircase leads up to the tower room but the walls have started to crumble and the Five have to take great care when going to the top of the tower. Downstairs in the largest of the four rooms is the entrance to a secret passage leading to a store-room once used by wreckers. The children learn about the tower from Grandad, whose father was a Wrecker. He tells them that the light from the tower can only be seen from one spot inland and that on wild and windy nights the light can still sometimes be seen.

MR LUFFY'S FRUITCAKE

With anything like a fruit cake there's always a 'certain something' which no recipe can give you, so do try to have the GOOD COOK of the family hovering nearby! If Mr Luffy – a teacher at the boys school – had made his own cake, the mixed fruit would probably have ended up as a solid mass at the bottom, or perhaps the cake would have more resembled a Christmas pudding.

What you will need:

100g/4oz butter (or good margarine)
200g/8oz self raising flour
100g/4oz caster sugar
100g/4oz mixed dried fruit
1 standard egg
1 teaspoon finely grated lemon rind
5 tablespoons milk
½ teaspoon mixed spice
A greased and lined tin (15cm/6in round)

What you do:

1. Sift the flour into a mixing bowl.

2. Rub the butter or margarine finely into the flour until your mixture resembles breadcrumbs.

3. Stir in the spice, sugar, lemon rind and mixed fruit until they are evenly distributed. (It's a good idea to have an older person watching you.)

4. Now beat the milk and egg together and add to your prepared mixture, stirring these in with a spoon until you have an evenly mixed dough.

5. Transfer the mixture to your tin.

6. Place the tin in the middle of a moderate oven (160°C or Gas Mark 3) and bake for 1 ¼ to 1 ½ hours (or until a thick skewer, inserted in the centre, comes out cleanly).

7. Remove from the oven and leave in the tin for a few minutes. Then turn out onto a wire tray to cool.

8. Remove the paper by peeling off carefully.

9. When cold, store your cake in an airtight tin.

Mr Luffy's cake should be enough for eight people.

WHICH CHARACTER ARE YOU?

The Famous Five all have strong, different personalities. Who are you most like?
Try this quiz and find out ...

1 What quality do you most admire?
1 – Humour
2 – Independence
3 – Good manners
4 – Loyalty
5 – Courage
6 – Kindness

2 What item would you take to a desert island (assuming you already had basic supplies)?
1 – A length of rope
2 – A favourite picture or ornament
3 – A big bar of chocolate
4 – A portable radio
5 – Hairdressing scissors
6 – A tin of biscuits

3 What is your attitude to adventures?
1 – You like to take charge and make decisions
2 – You hate to be left out of the action
3 – You'd rather read about them than have them
4 – You let others take the lead but you play your part willingly
5 – Crooks are more frightened of you than you are of them!
6 – Your life has been one long adventure!

4 How do you feel about food?
1 – You enjoy your meals but don't like having to prepare them
2 – You love cooking and baking
3 – You're always grateful for a lovely meal
4 – You adore food and you're constantly hungry
5 – You like food but it doesn't take over your life
6 – You gulp down your meals so fast that you barely taste them!

5 What's your favourite animal?
1 – A tiger
2 – A dog
3 – A monkey
4 – A lion
5 – A rabbit
6 – A snake

6 What would you do if you saw mysterious lights flashing from the top of a tower at midnight?
1 – Alert other members of the household
2 – Tremble with fear, wondering what was going on
3 – Slip out immediately to investigate
4 – Note down the pattern of the flashes as it might be a code
5 – Shin up the tower in a trice
6 – Arm yourself with a torch and a snack before slipping out to investigate

7 How might people describe you?
1 – Friendly
2 – Thoughtful
3 – Fierce
4 – Acrobatic or athletic
5 – Responsible
6 – Strong-willed

8 What career would you choose?
1 – A teacher
2 – An actor or performer of some kind
3 – A zookeeper
4 – A doctor
5 – A scientist
6 – A security guard

Scoring
Now check which letter is linked to each of your answers
(A, B, C, D, E or F) and see which letter comes up most for you.

1: 1 = C, 2 = B, 3 = D, 4 = E, 5 = A, 6 = F
2: 1 = F, 2 = A, 3 = C, 4 = D, 5 = B, 6 = E
3: 1 = D, 2 = B, 3 = A, 4 = C, 5 = E, 6 = F
4: 1 = B, 2 = A, 3 = F, 4 = C, 5 = D, 6 = E
5: 1 = A, 2 = B, 3 = C, 4 = D, 5 = E, 6 = F
6: 1 = E, 2 = A, 3 = B, 4 = D, 5 = F, 6 = C
7: 1 = C, 2 = A, 3 = E, 4 = F, 5 = D, 6 = B
8: 1 = A, 2 = F, 3 = B, 4 = C, 5 = D, 6 = E

Turn over the page to find out which letter represents which character.

ANSWERS

WHICH FAMOUS FIVE BOOK SHOULD I READ NEXT?

Mostly As – The book for you is *Five Go Off in a Caravan*! An idyllic holiday in horse-drawn caravans leads to unexpected danger and drama involving a circus.

Mostly Bs – The book for you is *Five Go to Demon's Rocks*! Staying in a lighthouse is exciting enough, but when the Five investigate tales of wreckers and hidden treasure, things become electrifying.

Mostly Cs – The book for you is *Five Go to Smuggler's Top*! After encountering strange goings-on in a quaint old town surrounded by misty marshes, the Five start to suspect that smugglers may not be confined to the pages of history books.

Mostly Ds – The book for you is *Five Go Off to Camp*! The wild and lonely moors hold plenty of secrets, but none more mysterious than the tale of a 'spook train' which runs at night... and vanishes!

Mostly Es – The book for you is *Five on Finniston Farm*! The Five are touched by the plight of a farming family who are going through a tough time, but can they help by uncovering a half-forgotten secret?

A mixture of letters
If it's a tie between two or more letters, just choose the title which appeals to you most – or read both/all the relevant books!

WHAT'S WRONG?

1. Aeroplane – no tail.
2. Upper tent – no tent pole.
3. Deck chair – no supporting strut.
4. Hen swimming.
5. Kettle – no spout.
6. Table – three legs.
7. Boy holding jug wrong way round.
8. Boy's jacket buttons on wrong side.
9. Boy in the deck chair – one long trouser leg and one short.

A LADDER TO A 'BADDIE'!

GRAND	LACES	ROOKY
BRAND	LACKS	PULL
BLAND	LOCKS	POLL
BLANK	ROCKS	POOL
BLACK	ROOKS	WOOL
BLOCK		WOOH

FIVE GET INTO A FIX FIND-A-WORD

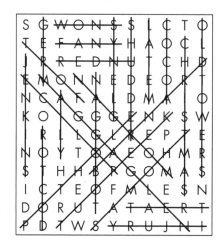

FIVE GO DOWN TO THE SEA WORD CROSS

Across: 2. Disappeared, 5. Church, 7. Barnies, 9. Guvnor, 10. Sweets, 12. Nellie, 13. Cliff, 15. Sinister, 16. Way.

Down: 1. Hearth, 3. Smuggle, 4. Willy, 5. Cornwall, 6. Caves, 8. Polpenny, 11. Filthy, 14. Farm, 15. Sid.

FIENDISH FAMOUS FIVE QUIZ ANSWERS

1. Jake.
2. To discuss his plans for draining the marshes that surround Castaway Hill.
3. He makes wooden toys.
4. Coney is another word for rabbit.
5. Timmy.
6. Tremannon Farm.
7. Curly (because of his curly tail).
8. They get a ride back in a police car.
9. Pops.
10. Aily.
11. Lucas.
12. Secret signs, often made from twigs or leaves, left by gypsies to give other gypsies a message.
13. In a cave they find on the shore near the wreck.
14. She climbs up the ivy that covers the tower wall.
15. She likes to squirt water over people with her trunk.
16. Carters Lane.
17. Ben.
18. Sid.
19. A long splinter of wood flies off the door and imbeds itself in his cheek.
20. Gloomy Water.

WHICH CHARACTER ARE YOU?

Mostly As
You're Anne! Kind and considerate, you always think of others' feelings and that makes people warm to you. Because you tend to be cautious, some people might get the impression that you're timid. However, you can be extremely brave when necessary. You're also efficient and organised, which your friends and family appreciate.

Mostly Bs
You're George! Independent and spirited, you have strong views and will go your own way rather than following the crowd. Some people might regard you as stubborn, but others would say you're steadfast. You might not always find it easy to make friends, but any friends you do make find that you stick up for them and are there for them through thick and thin. You love adventurous activities and expeditions, and hate to be left out of the action.

Mostly Cs
You're Dick! You're friendly and have a terrific sense of humour, and people enjoy your company. Although you love a joke, you have a more serious and sensitive side as well. You're full of good ideas and you revel in adventures – as long as there is plenty to eat!

Mostly Ds
You're Julian! You are a natural leader, sensible and reliable, and people trust you with positions of responsibility. You're intelligent, good at problem-solving and take life seriously – but don't forget to let your hair down from time to time and have some fun!

Mostly Es
You're Timmy! Okay, so Timmy is a dog! Nevertheless, he has some admirable qualities which are good to find in a human too. Like Timmy, you are full of energy and eager for adventure. You are loyal to your friends and will do all you can to help them in times of difficulty or danger. You can be fierce when provoked, but you have a gentle side as well.

Mostly Fs
You're Jo, who appears in the ninth, eleventh and fourteenth Famous Five books! You're up for a challenge and keen to do your bit. Practical, brave and very active, you are fun to have around and you always have something useful to contribute. Sometimes you can be impulsive, rushing in without stopping to think, so don't forget to look before you leap!

A mixture of letters
If it's a tie between two or more letters, that means you're a mixture of several characters and should read the descriptions for both/all the relevant characters.